BEHIND THE MASK

JEFF GOTTESFELD

SADDLEBACK
EDUCATIONAL PUBLISHING

WHITE LIGHTNING BOOKS

SADDLEBACK
EDUCATIONAL PUBLISHING
www.sdlback.com

ISBN-13: 978-1-68021-142-9
ISBN-10: 1-68021-142-0
eBook: 978-1-63078-542-0

Printed in Malaysia

21 20 19 18 17   1 2 3 4 5

ABOUT 8TH GRADE

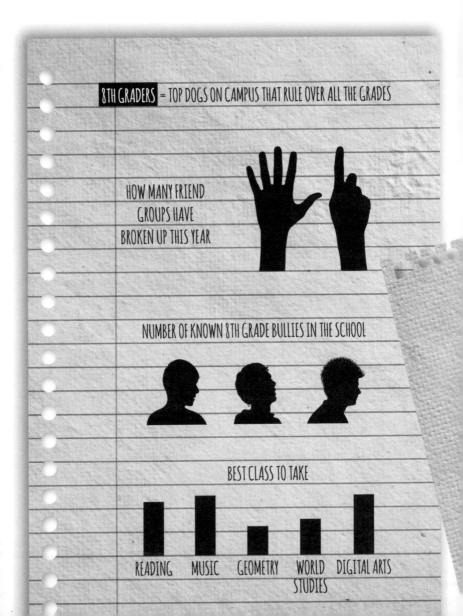

8TH GRADERS = TOP DOGS ON CAMPUS THAT RULE OVER ALL THE GRADES

HOW MANY FRIEND
GROUPS HAVE
BROKEN UP THIS YEAR

NUMBER OF KNOWN 8TH GRADE BULLIES IN THE SCHOOL

BEST CLASS TO TAKE

READING   MUSIC   GEOMETRY   WORLD   DIGITAL ARTS
                             STUDIES

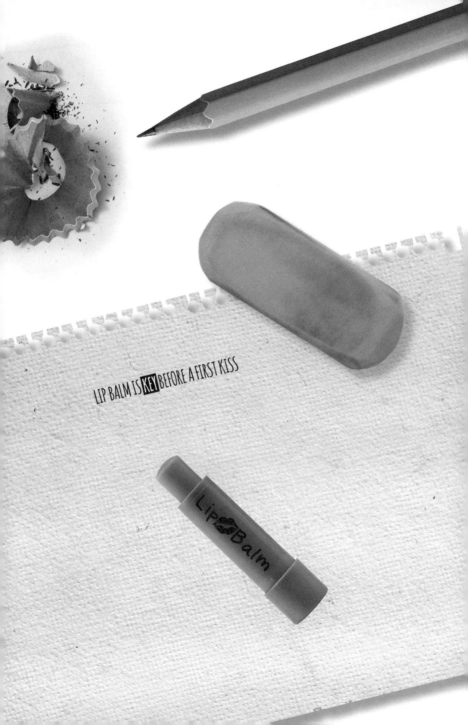

LIP BALM IS KEY BEFORE A FIRST KISS

CHAPTER 1

I LOVE YOU

Serena Smith watched her new boyfriend. His name was Kai Lambert. Kai stood at the frozen yogurt shop's cash register. She still couldn't believe it. Kai had wanted her to be his girlfriend.

Serena was the new girl in town. Her family had moved in August. It was unexpected. Serena's grandma was sick. Her mom wanted to be close. She would take care of her. They moved one thousand miles northeast. It meant Serena had to start a new school for eighth grade. She was happy that her grandma was cared for. But it wasn't fun to be the new girl.

It wasn't fun. But then Kai had come up to her in study hall. Tall. Long hair. A smile that could light up the night. He was popular. And the dude played a mean guitar. Everyone liked Kai.

Serena had never been anything too great at her old school. She was cute enough. Nice enough. Smart enough. But she was never a girl with any power. Now, with Kai? She had a little power. Everyone she'd invited to her upcoming Halloween party had said yes.

She was at the yogurt shop today. It was called Blizz. A bunch of new friends were with her. With Kai as her boyfriend, it wasn't hard to make friends. They came to her.

She even had a new best friend. Her name was April Frost. April slid into the seat next to her. "Omigod. Look at Kai. Paying for your yogurt. My old boyfriend never paid for me."

"Yeah." Serena grinned. Kai always bought

her frozen yogurt. He held doors open. He stood when she entered a room. It made her feel like a million bucks.

He came back and gave her the cup of frozen yogurt. He'd put nuts on it. That was just how she liked it. "Talking about the party?" he asked.

"Not yet. We were waiting on you."

"All I want to do is put on a costume. Show up," Kai said. "That's big for me. I leave the rest in your hands." He turned to his friends at the next table. "I'm right, right? The girls plan the party. Then the guys just show up. Right?"

His guy friends laughed. The girls grinned good-naturedly. Serena thought this was unfair. They'd do the work. But then the guys would have the fun. The idea of letting guys plan a party wasn't good either. They'd mess it up. Anyway, there were a few weeks until Halloween. There was plenty of time to set things up.

"What's your costume going to be?" April asked Serena.

"Serena's going to be a baby doll," Kai joked.

Serena kicked him lightly on the shin. "Not funny."

Troy snorted. He was Kai's best friend.

April's phone sounded with a text. She checked it. "It's my mom. She wants me home." She gave her phone a shake. "Serena, I'll call you."

When April left, so did the other girls. Troy and the guys took off too. Now it was just Kai and Serena. She liked it. It felt more like a date this way.

He spooned up some frozen yogurt. Then held it up. She opened her mouth. He slid the spoon in. It was such a romantic thing to do. Serena turned her head to the left. An older woman was watching them.

"Ain't love grand?" the lady said.

Serena nodded. "It is when you have the best guy. Which I do."

Kai put his arm around her. "You heard what she said. Love is grand."

Serena felt herself blush. She was glad she had darker skin and hair. Her blush wouldn't show as much. Kai had never said that he loved her. They'd only been a couple for a month. They were just in eighth grade. It was pretty young to talk about love. But still.

"It sure is," she told him. She boldly took hold of his right hand.

"Did I tell you yet that I love you?" he said softly. "Since I do."

Wow!

There they were. The three magic words. *I love you*. He had spoken them.

From any guy that would mean a lot. From the coolest guy at the school? Serena felt like the luckiest girl in the world.

She knew what she had to do. She leaned toward his right ear.

"I love you too," she said softly.

Now they'd both said it. It was just three words. But those words changed things. The words made their feelings stronger. Deeper. A couple that would last.

"Hey. You guys look so happy!"

The voice had come from behind them. Serena turned. It was a guy their age. He wore jeans and a T-shirt. He was skinny. The guy had round glasses like Harry Potter. They were cool on Harry Potter. On this guy they looked kind of silly. She wanted to be nice, though.

"Thanks," she told him. "We are."

The guy ignored her. He zeroed in on Kai. "Hey. It's so good to see you. How you been? It's been a long time."

Kai looked at him blankly. "Do we know each other?"

"We sure do, Kai. Ollie?" said the guy. "It's Ollie! How you doing? How's it going?"

Huh? The new guy knew Kai. Or at least he knew his name. Who was he?

Serena looked at Kai. Waited to see what he'd say next. He could not be more blunt. "Ollie?

I don't know an Ollie. I'm not sure I want to know an Ollie."

Serena saw the guy wince. His feelings had been hurt. Kai didn't know him. He was telling the truth. Her boyfriend did not lie.

CHAPTER 2

ODDBALL

The guy in the Harry Potter glasses didn't give up.

"Come on, Kai. Don't be like that. It's Ollie. You know. From Miss Posner's class? First grade? Wilson School?"

Ah. Now it made sense to Serena. Kai and Ollie had once been in the same class. It had been a long time ago. Kai just didn't remember. She spoke up. "I'm Serena. I wasn't in that class. I just moved here."

"Well, you're with a great guy. Kai is the real deal," Ollie said.

Kai still looked confused. "Are you sure, man? We were in the same class? Maybe you're thinking of someone else."

Ollie nodded. "Of course I'm sure. You and Troy were buds then. You still friends now?"

Serena wanted to be nice. "They're still friends. Kai, think back. You guys were in the same class. Why don't you join us, Ollie?"

"Yeah, man. Sit down." Kai seemed to relax. "You know, it's coming back to me. Ollie … Ollie … Sorry, dude. I don't remember your last name."

Ollie sat in the chair where April had been. He seemed eager to please. "Kidd. Ollie Kidd."

"That's right! Of course." Kai smacked himself in the forehead with his palm. "Ollie Kidd. What happened to you?"

Ollie grinned. "It's a long story."

He shared the short version. Ollie had left the school after first grade. In fact, he had left town. He had free spirit parents who bought a motor home. His dad was an author. His mom wrote a blog. They lived on the road. His parents had home-schooled him. Now they were back in town for a while.

"That's great," Serena said. It was kind of cool to meet someone else who knew Kai back in first grade. "Are you coming back to school?"

Ollie shook his head gravely. "Uh, no. Regular school and me? We never really got along."

"What about friends? How can you make friends if you don't go to regular school?" Serena asked.

"I'm fine. I do okay by myself," Ollie said.

"Maybe we can be your friends," Serena said. "Right, Kai?"

"Um, sure," Kai declared.

Ollie put his hand on Kai's shoulder. "Where'd this girl come from? Because she could give lessons in how to be nice." He checked his phone for the time. "I gotta go. I've got a dog that needs a walk." He stood and put out his hand to Serena.

It felt a little formal and odd. Whatever. She shook it. "It's good to meet you, Serena."

Serena also stood. "Good to meet you too, Ollie. See you around."

Kai sat there. Finally, he stood too. "Yeah. Good to see you again, Ollie. Take care, dude."

They watched him leave. He had a funny walk. He moved his hands out to his sides, like he needed to balance. Kai grinned.

"Same old oddball," he told Serena.

"Excuse me?"

"That was the dude's nickname. Oliver *Oddball*." Kai laughed. "He walked the same way in first grade." Kai did a version of the Ollie walk. It was so on-target that strangers in Blizz laughed. Serena laughed a little too. Kai's imitation was both mean and funny.

"Maybe we should invite him to the Halloween party," she said. "I mean, that would be a nice thing. Wouldn't it?"

Kai howled. "The Halloween party? Are you

kidding? Ollie Oddball at your Halloween party? Serena, trust me. You don't want him at your party. You just don't. Come on. Let's go."

They left Blizz. Serena only lived ten minutes away. Kai walked her all the way home. On the doorstep he took her by the arms. "You were really kind to Ollie. You are a nice person. You know that?"

She nodded, hoping he would kiss her. "I try to be."

Then her mother opened the door. Darn it! No first kiss. It was like the kiss alarm had gone off in her mom's head.

She thought about the kiss that might have been all night. And she didn't think about Ollie Oddball.

INTO THE WOODS

Serena liked to walk her dog. His name was Toots. Toots was a yellow lab. Serena had rescued him from the pound. He was a great dog. Toots chased balls. He did tricks. The dog barked at bad strangers. He could sense nice people. At first Toots had barked at Kai. That was because Kai had allergies.

Some kids were not good with taking care of their pets. Serena was not one of those kids. She did three dog walks a day. Each walk was for twenty minutes. She brushed him. She fed him. She let him sleep on her bed.

The move had been hard. It would have been much harder if not for Toots. He loved the new place. There were fresh sights and smells. It wasn't like Texas. There was a real autumn here. Leaves piled up in the streets. Acorns littered the sidewalks. Toots couldn't wait to go out and play.

Serena took a long walk with Toots on Saturday morning. She was still learning the area. She took a street they had not been on before. At the end of it was a wooded area. They went into the woods. The path was narrow. It was covered in pine needles. The air smelled fresh and clean.

Serena took Toots off the leash. He ran ahead. Then started to bark. Serena went to see what he was barking at. She grinned. He had found a small pond. There were ducks floating on the water. Toots ran back and forth, barking. The ducks took off into the air. Toots looked sadly at Serena.

"What do you want me to do?" she asked him. "I didn't tell you to—"

"Hey! Hey, Serena!"

Someone was calling her name. She peered into the trees and saw no one. That gave her the chills. Who was out there?

Then she heard her name again. "Serena!"

Her heart pounded. The person could see her. But she couldn't see him. Then she caught sight of who it was.

Ollie Kidd. *Oddball.* What was he doing in the woods?

Serena had a scary thought. Ollie had followed her. Worse, he was stalking her.

Toots saw Ollie too. The dog ran to him. No barking, though. Instead, he danced around happily. He liked him. That made Serena feel better. Toots had never made a mistake with people. At least not yet. Still. This was too unlikely. This wasn't Main Street. This was the woods.

"Ollie," she said. "What are you doing here?"

"Oh, this is the best shortcut. Our house is on Warwick. I come this way all the time. You live near here?"

She nodded. "Yeah. On Downing. Seven fifty-five. What about you?"

"Warwick is just a block over. I guess we're going to see each other around." He kneeled to pet Toots. "I think I told you I've got a dog too. Petey. He's a mutt. And he's pretty cool. Hey! Maybe we could do some walks together."

Serena nodded. It felt off, talking to Ollie here by the pond. It just didn't make sense. Even if Ollie lived a block over from her. What were the chances they'd be in the woods at the same time? She couldn't shake the feeling that he had followed her.

"You have your phone?" Ollie asked.

That was an odd question. Was it just a trick? Did he not want her to call for help?

"Yeah," Serena said nervously.

"Then take my number. In case you want to set up a dog walk."

Serena couldn't really say no. They swapped digits. Ollie kept petting Toots. Toots still seemed to like him. Then there was silence.

"Know what would be fun?" Ollie finally asked.

"What?"

"If you and me and Kai could go out sometime," Ollie said. "To a movie or something. I was thinking about it. Now that I'm back. It'd be cool to make friends with you guys. What do you think?"

Serena thought it would be cool to get out of the woods. Now. As for going out with Ollie and Kai? They could talk about it another time. She got why he wanted to hang out with them. She knew what it was like to try to fit in.

Kai was cool. She might still be an outsider without him. For Ollie it might be even harder. He had that nickname. Did he know other kids called him that? Probably. People always knew the things that hurt them.

"Talk to Kai about it," Ollie said.

"I will," Serena said. It seemed the best way to end the meeting.

"Okay, see ya."

Ollie turned. He headed back the way he had come. Serena thought that was odd too. He'd said he was cutting through the woods. Was that even true? It was a weird way to do it.

CHAPTER 4

THE BASKET

That afternoon, April came over. April was super smart. She wrote poetry. Kai wrote music from some of her poems. April had grown up in town. The girl knew everyone. She was also gorgeous. She had long blonde hair, blue eyes, and the cutest freckles on her nose.

April and Serena did Sudoku for a while. Then they talked about the Halloween party. April had promised she would help. They decided to bring in pizzas. There would be a costume contest. Everyone could vote on the best costume.

"What if someone doesn't wear a costume?" April asked. "What do you want to do?"

"Hmm. Good question. Pour chocolate sauce on them?" Serena joked.

"That'd be messy."

Serena thought for a moment. "I say we can have masks. Like, kiddie masks. Princesses and princes. No one would want that. So everyone will wear costumes instead."

April nodded. "I like that idea. What's your costume going to be?"

"I have a choice," Serena said. "Check this out."

She took April to her closet. Serena liked acting in plays. She'd kept all her costumes from her old shows. There was one of a pirate. One of a mushroom too. And one where she had been a red devil.

"Go with the sparkling devil," April said. "Can I maybe use that pirate one?"

For the next few minutes, they tried on costumes. April decided the pirate costume was great. She wanted a mask to go with it. "What about Kai? What's he going to wear?"

Serena shrugged. "I have no idea."

"You'd better be on his case," April said. "He never dresses up for Halloween."

"Really?"

April nodded. "Really. I remember first grade. There was a costume parade. It was a big thing for all us kids. Kai showed up in jeans and a T-shirt. He said costumes were dumb. No way was he going to wear one."

Serena wanted to know something. Maybe April could fill her in.

"April? What was Kai like back then?"

April looked at her oddly. "That's a strange question."

Serena smiled. "I'm a strange girl. Humor me. I wasn't here. I want to know."

"Why don't you just ask him?"

Serena laughed. "Ask a guy in eighth grade what he was like in first grade? That's expecting a lot of self-awareness. Weren't you two in the same class?"

April nodded. "Yeah. But I don't remember much. Girls hang with girls when they're little. Boys are mostly pests. I wrote a poem about it."

"You must remember something about him," Serena pressed.

April snapped her fingers. "He was the best at sports. I remember that."

Serena wasn't interested in his hobbies. A frown crossed her face. "What kind of person was he?"

"Well, he was always kind of—"

Just then the doorbell rang. Serena's mom and dad were raking leaves out back. She was the only one around to answer.

"Hold that thought," she said. "Let's see who's at the door."

They went downstairs together. The doorbell sounded again.

"Coming!" Serena called.

They were at the door a few seconds later. No one was there. But there was a gift basket. It was on the porch. Wow! There was a lot of stuff.

"Welcome Wagon," April said.

"Welcome *what?*"

"It's like a club for old ladies. They bring stuff to newcomers. Baskets like this. My mom used to work with them."

Serena frowned again. "Kind of late, isn't it? We've been here two months."

April shrugged. "Let's check it out."

They went to the basket. April was right. It was a welcome package. There were menus from restaurants. A guide of fun things to do in town. A few gift certificates. Even a map that showed all the town parks. But there was more. Serena opened an envelope. There were three movie tickets to the local multiplex. There was a handwritten note in the envelope too.

Serena,

It was fun seeing you in the woods today. You're going to really like it here. I made this basket for you. I know you don't know the town well. There are also three movie tickets. You can use them to go to the movies with me and a friend of your choice. Hint.

See you soon!

Ollie

April read the note over her shoulder. "Ollie gave that to you? How does he even know where you live?"

Serena sighed. "It's a long story. And kind of creepy."

April smiled. "I love creepy."

Serena told April the story. How she had met up with Ollie in the woods. The story was so weird. And now it felt creepy to the max.

CHAPTER 5

DOG PARK

Serena could not believe what she was doing. No way was it her idea. Her parents had insisted. She had to thank Ollie for the gift basket. She didn't really want to. But she did what they asked. Serena texted Ollie a simple thank you.

He had texted back.

OLLIE: (Welcome!)

Then he had asked a question. Did she want to see

a really cool dog park? It was about a half mile away. He could meet her there. And he could bring his own dog, Petey.

OLLIE: Who knows? Petey and Toots could fall in luv.

Okay. That was funny. Serena couldn't help but grin.

SERENA: Really? They're both boys.

OLLIE: Hey. It's the 21st century. Who are we to get in the way?

It was a good comeback. Serena said yes to meeting him. They decided to go on Sunday morning. Serena didn't tell Kai. She didn't want his disapproval. Plus it would be great for Toots. He could make a doggy friend.

It turned out to be an awesome dog park. There

were slides. There was a splash pool. There were big tubes. The dogs could run through them. It was a playground. For dogs! There was even a grassy area. People could throw balls and discs. Dogs could chase them. Toots loved to chase balls. Serena found a flinger and a ball. She launched one about fifty yards. Toots barked happily and chased it.

"Some dog!" she heard from behind her.

There was Ollie. With him was the fattest dog Serena had ever seen. He was part dachshund. Most dogs of that breed looked like hot dogs. Petey looked like a burrito.

"He's … kind of big."

"Yeah," Ollie said. "Petey's a little on the chub side."

"How about a diet?"

"Nah. He likes Taco Bell too much."

Toots came running back with the ball. He spotted Petey. Toots slowed. Then he approached with caution. The two dogs sniffed each other. Serena watched carefully. She was ready to jump in at any sign of trouble. There was none. It only took seconds. The two dogs ran around like they'd known each other forever.

Serena and Ollie found a bench. They sat and watched the action. There was plenty to see. There had to be fifty other dogs in the park.

The two had a chance to talk. To her surprise, Ollie turned out to be charming. He liked computer games and cooking. He took great pictures with his phone. All the dogs in the park loved him. She told him about the plays she had been in. Shared how hard it was to be the new kid.

"At least you're with Kai," he said. "That's gotta help."

"It does. A lot. I wonder sometimes. What would it be like not to be with him?"

He made a face. "You'd have less friends."

"I guess that's true."

"Well, you're with him. Don't worry about it," he said. "So. We know each other better now.

You'll ask Kai about the movies?" He winked. "The tickets won't cost anything."

There was something she had to ask. "How come you're so into the idea?"

"I like to see how people change." His eyes got a faraway look. "I moved around so much. Didn't really get to know anyone. Make friends."

"Okay," she said.

The smile on Ollie's face lit up the day. He resettled his glasses. "That's great!"

Serena's doubts were gone. Ollie was fine. Kai had a ton of friends. Serena had only been in town for a couple of months. She had a few friends. But she and Kai hadn't made a friend together.

Maybe Ollie could be that friend.

It was Sunday evening. Kai and Serena were downtown. Food trucks came to the town square. They'd decided to eat there. They had just picked up fish tacos. Kai had brought his guitar. They found a good place on the grass. Serena had told him all about what had happened with Ollie. The woods, the gift basket, the movie tickets, and then her visit to the dog park.

"Don't you get it, Serena? He likes you. Like, *likes* you."

"It isn't like that," Serena said.

Kai's laugh was cynical. "It definitely is like that. He met you in the woods. How do you think that happened? He gives you a gift basket. Why do you think he did that? He invites you on a doggie date. You show up. You decide you like him. It all happens fast. You're a hot girl, Serena. Now be a smart hot girl."

Serena didn't want Kai to think she had any ideas about Ollie. "Come on. It isn't like that. I don't like him that way."

Kai laughed again. "You don't have to. He likes you enough that way for both of you. Hey. Taste this."

He lifted the taco to her lips. She bit into it. It was savory and hot.

"Love, love, love," Serena declared.

"Exactly. That's what your boy Ollie Oddball wants you to say to him."

It was a crisp fall night. The sun was already setting. It made Serena think about the Halloween party. It would be great to have a bonfire. She didn't even know if that was legal. She wanted to invite Ollie. But then she dropped the idea. She didn't mind that Kai seemed jealous. No guy had ever been jealous of her before. It had to mean he really liked her.

Then Kai said something that surprised her. "Maybe it isn't a bad idea for us three to hang out."

"Really?"

"Yeah," Kai said. "He'll see that I'm with you and you're with me. Then he'll back off. If he has any sense. Let's set something up."

"We have those movie tickets. He got them for us."

Kai shook his head. "A movie sounds like a long ordeal. How about we just go to Blizz? Hang out there. That should be enough."

He took his guitar from the case. Then he got a pick and ran off some blues notes. Serena watched his fingers fly. She had no talent at music. Kai was loaded with talent. Again, she felt lucky to be with him.

He finished the song. "I wrote that this afternoon. Know what it's called?"

"No clue," Serena said.

"'Serena's Song,'" he told her.

Serena swooned. He had written music for her. That was about the most romantic thing in the world. She'd boldly leaned in and kissed him on the cheek. "Thank you."

He touched her under the chin. Then he held his lips up to hers. A moment later Serena got her first real kiss.

Swoon.

CHAPTER 6

THE MOVIES

Serena got busy. She and April planned the Halloween party. Serena decided she would wait to hang with Ollie and Kai at Blizz. She didn't text Ollie. He didn't text her either.

The week went by. There was no school on Friday. Some kind of teacher in-service thing. She and her friends went to the movies on Thursday night. There was a new horror flick called *Fright*. It was about a boy who moved into an old house with his family. He found a monster living under the stairs. The monster fell in love with him. Then it got jealous of the boy's girlfriend. It wanted to kill them both. Serena didn't usually like scary movies. But to be with her friends, holding Kai's hand, screaming at the bloody parts? That was her idea of a good time.

When the movie was over, the kids headed for the lobby. She made her way up the aisle.

"Serena?"

She flushed at the voice. It was Ollie. He was a few seats in, to her left. Ollie was alone. She had a choice. She could act like she hadn't heard. Or she could stop and talk. But she didn't know what to say. He had wanted to go to the movies with them. He had even paid for the tickets. Here she was at the movies. But she was with her other friends. Not with Ollie.

He had to feel bad about it.

"Hey," she said.

"Hey. What the hell? I thought you were going to call me." He sounded hurt. "I really wanted to see this movie with you and Kai. Now you're here anyway? What gives?"

"Serena! Come on! Kai's waiting for you." April was up ahead of her. "We're leaving!"

Behind April, someone sang, "Odd-ball. Odd-BALL. Odd-*BALL*."

"Hold on," she told Ollie. "I'll be back."

Serena marched up the aisle to see who was making fun of Ollie. There was no reason to be mean. It was Kai's friend, Troy.

"Chill," she warned him.

"Chill what?" he asked.

"You're teasing Ollie. I don't like it."

Troy made a face at her. "You have no idea who you're dealing with. That guy's going to be an ax murderer some day."

Serena looked around. "Where's Kai?"

"Restroom," Troy told her. "Why don't you go suck face with Oddball?"

Whoa. That was cold. Serena got really mad. "Why don't *you* go suck face with the mirror?

Because that's the only way you'll ever find someone to touch you."

She marched back down the aisle. She hoped
Ollie was still there. She wanted him to see that
she had defended him. But he was gone.

CHAPTER 7

THE "DATE"

It was finally happening. Serena saw Kai in the lobby after the movie. She told him Troy had made fun of Ollie. Could they go out with Ollie? Soon?

"You've got clout," she'd told Kai. "The other kids need to know the three of us are friends. Then they won't tease him anymore."

"Okay. I want to make you happy. Set it up," he said. "Blizz. Wednesday. After school."

Serena did. Ollie was thrilled.

On Wednesday they walked over from school. Ollie had beaten them there. Blizz had good Internet. He was on his laptop. He grinned and waved as they came through the door. He wore jeans and a red long-sleeve shirt. Serena had on a cute black skirt and silk top. Kai wore a Packers jersey and black pants.

"Hey, look what I found!" Ollie pointed to his computer screen.

"Let us get some froyo first, man. Then we'll check it out," Kai said.

Kai and Serena each got cups of frozen yogurt. They put on their favorite toppings.

Ollie had a frozen yogurt shake. He seemed really excited. He could barely sit still. "Look what I dug up!" He spun his computer around so they could see. It was a class picture from first grade. The teacher, Miss Posner, was in the middle. She was pretty old.

Serena looked at the picture closely. She picked out Kai right away. He was a smaller version of eighth-grade Kai. There was April too. Her hair was extra blonde. And Troy. Plus a few other kids she knew. She had to hunt around to find Ollie. He was in the bottom row.

Everyone else in the class had regular hair. Ollie had a buzz cut. He wore glasses. They weren't Harry Potter style. They were oval, with thick rims. His shirt was buttoned to the very top. He didn't smile at the camera. Instead, he scowled.

She looked over at Kai. He smiled wryly. She could tell what he was thinking: *Oddball!*

"What was it like? First grade, I mean," Serena asked. She wanted to be friendly.

She saw Ollie's eyes flash at Kai. Then he looked away. "It was okay. It's better being home-schooled."

Kai nodded. "Word, dude. I wished I'd been home-schooled too."

Serena had never heard Kai say that before. "Why do you say that, Kai?"

"Sleep as late as you want? Do a whole day of

school in a few hours? That sounds like the life. I bet it's the life. Right, Ollie?"

Ollie's eyebrows wrinkled. "It wasn't all good. It was hard to make friends."

"That's because you were going from place to place," Kai said.

"I didn't have many friends in first grade," Ollie said.

"That was a long time ago," Kai told him.

"Yeah, I guess," Ollie said.

For the next few minutes, they slurped their treats. Ollie stared into his shake. Serena felt bad for him. He'd been such an outsider back then. She wondered if there was a way to make it different now.

"Ollie? Why don't you think about coming to school?" she asked him. "I mean, kids come in all the time. You could just enroll. You'd make friends. I know you would."

"No way. I'm never going back to public school." Ollie looked oddly at Kai. Serena wondered what that was about.

"Think about it," Serena said. "We'll be your friend. Right, Kai?"

"For sure." Kai couldn't have sounded more sincere.

Ollie shook his head. "Nah. I don't think so. Hey. Want to see some pictures from when I was traveling?"

For the next half hour, Serena and Kai looked at Ollie's pictures. He had an endless supply on his computer. At first it was cool to see the Grand Canyon. Then some of the national parks. After ten minutes it got kind of old. After twenty minutes it got really old. And at the end of a half hour, Serena felt like her butt had merged with the seat.

At first she'd tried to comment on each picture. After a while, she just shut up. Ollie didn't seem to get the hint.

"And this one is at Big Bend. It's in Texas," he told them. "We just …"

His voice trailed off.

Oops! Serena was checking out some high

school kids across the yogurt shop. Kai's eyes had closed.

"You guys aren't listening!" Ollie said.

Serena felt bad. But a half hour of someone else's photos would bore anyone. It wouldn't matter whose photos they were. Nicki Minaj. Boring. Taylor Swift. Boring.

"Sorry, dude," Kai said.

"Yeah, sorry," Serena muttered.

Ollie stood. He snapped his computer closed with a bang. "You know what? Nothing ever changes. Nothing!"

He put the computer under his arm. Then he stormed out of the shop. Kai turned to Serena. A slow smile spread over his face.

"See? Once an oddball? Always an oddball."

Serena couldn't disagree.

CHAPTER 8

THE WOODS AGAIN

Later that afternoon Serena took Toots for his walk. He had come to loves the woods. As soon as they left the house, he always pulled toward them. Serena liked to take him there at least once a day. But this walk couldn't be too long. She was going to April's house in forty-five minutes. Her mom would give her a lift. She decided to take the dog up to the pond and back. That would be about a thirty-minute walk.

The trees were so pretty. All the leaves had

now changed color. There were maples with their bright red leaves. The oaks with their golden yellows. The wind made the leaves flutter. They shimmered on their branches. One good rainstorm would bring them down. Winter wasn't far away. For now, it was amazing. Toots loved it. He ran from tree to tree. Then he chased a rabbit. It ran out of sight into some bushes.

That's when Serena heard her name.

"Hey! Serena! Hey!"

She knew the voice. Ollie. She shuddered. He was coming toward her. Petey was with him. But how had he known again that she'd be in the woods?

"Hey," she said warily. "What … what are you doing here?"

"Walking Petey. Sorry about Blizz. I got a little carried away with the pictures."

"It's okay. Have a nice walk." She called to Toots. Her dog was over at the edge of the pond. "Come on, Toots. We're out of here."

"Why are you leaving?" Ollie asked. "I really want to talk to you."

Serena bit her lower lip. They'd just seen each other at Blizz. There'd been plenty of time to talk. She tried to be kind, but firm. "You know, Ollie? I don't really want to talk now. You asked to go out with Kai and me. It happened. Let's leave it there."

She started back toward the path. Toots followed her. She checked behind her to see if Ollie was following her. He wasn't. She was about a hundred feet away. Then she heard his voice call to her. It gave her chills.

"Talk to me, Serena! Or you're going to be sorry!"

Serena started to run. She didn't stop until she was home.

April's house was the nicest place she'd ever seen. It was huge. Modern. April's dad was a builder who had constructed it himself. Most of the walls were glass. The only strange part was the art.

April's mom was an artist. All her paintings were of the same thing. They were huge self-portraits. It meant April had to see her mom in every room.

"You get used to it," April said. It was Serena's first time there. April was giving her the tour. "After a while I don't even notice."

"Doesn't she ever paint anything else?"

April shook her head. "Nope. My dad loves it. Grownups are crazy. Let's go into the hot tub."

The house had a tub out back. Serena had brought her swimsuit. She changed and went outside. April was already in the water. Serena slid in. The hot water was heaven. No one could see the tub from the house. It was completely private.

"Sometimes at night? I'll skinny-dip," April said.

Serena made a face. "With Ollie around? I'm not skinny-dipping anywhere."

"Did something else happen with him?"

Serena slid all the way down. It soaked her hair. Ah. But the hot water took the tension out of her neck.

"Dunking is not an answer," April said.

"Yeah. Something happened." Serena told April the story of the afternoon. "He said in the woods I'd be sorry if I didn't talk to him. Should I be scared? Because I am."

The good news for Serena was that April didn't seem wigged out. "Nah. Don't be scared. That's just basic Ollie Oddball action."

"I think he's stalking me."

April shook her head. "He's not stalking you. He's just being Ollie."

"I could tell Kai to tell him to back off."

April leaned toward her. "Let it go. Ollie will back off on his own. He always does."

Serena nodded. "You know him better than I do. Okay." She tried to relax. But she wasn't convinced.

CHAPTER 9

ANOTHER BASKET

Serena slept late on Sunday morning. She awoke at ten. The house was empty. That was normal. Her folks liked to play tennis on Sundays. The cold weather was coming. Soon there wouldn't be many chances to play.

She stayed in bed for a while going over party plans. It would be on Friday night. All the invites were out. There would be thirty people. Everyone said they would come in costume. There would be a pumpkin-carving contest. Her mom would be the judge. They would serve pizza. There would be dancing. Kai said he would make a dance mix.

The party would end with a costume contest, then a bonfire. It had been cleared with the fire department. She hoped it would be the best Halloween party ever.

Serena was sleepy. She could use another hour being lazy. But the doorbell rang. Who could it be? She put on her robe and went downstairs. Serena opened the front door. There was a gift basket on the porch.

"Ugh. Not again," she muttered to herself. "Ollie!"

The basket was piled high with DVDs. Large boxes of candy spilled over the sides. There was a note on top. Her stomach did a flip-flop. She didn't want to read the note. She could predict what it would say.

Of course. The basket was from Ollie. She groaned as she unfolded the paper.

Dear Serena,

Hi. It's me. I am really sorry about yesterday. I am sorry if it freaked you out. I sometimes have a hard time knowing the right thing to do. I was so nervous at Blizz with you and Kai. I acted stupid. Showing you guys all those pictures was rude and thoughtless. Then I was scary in the woods. I'm sorry for that.

I'm awkward with people. I can't help it. I try my best. I thought that maybe you and Kai could be my real friends. But I don't know if I'm cut out to have a real friend. That's okay. I'll live. I always do. I'll just go on with my life. Tell Kai that I've forgiven everyone. I'm fine. Oh! I hear you're having a party for Halloween. This basket could make that party a lot better.

Have fun. Maybe we'll see each other walking our dogs or stuff. But I promise I won't talk to you. I swear it.

Ollie

Serena read the note a few times. Part of her was glad. Ollie was out of her life. But part of her was curious. Why tell Kai that Ollie had forgiven everyone? Was he talking about what happened in the theater? Serena thought so. But it felt like maybe it was something else. She decided to show the note to Kai. What would he have to say?

And what about all the candy and DVDs? Ollie had said they were for the party. The candy was awesome. But what about the DVDs? Serena got one at random. She put it into her laptop.

OMG. It was a slasher movie mix. No titles. No words. No sound. Just gory clips from bloody films. She shut it off. Were all the DVDs like that? She got a few others and played them. Yes. They were all the same. Different clips. High body counts.

Ollie was seriously out there.

That afternoon Serena went to an orchard. She was with Kai, April, Troy, and Troy's girlfriend, Megan. Before they went, Troy said sorry for being such a jerk at the movies. Serena accepted his apology. It was easier than being at odds with Kai's best bud.

They picked apples by the basket. The apples were red and crisp. Serena and April decided they would bob for apples at the party. It meant the masks had to come off. Oh well. It would be fun.

Serena and Kai were finally alone. She showed him the note from Ollie. "What's he talking about, 'I forgive everyone'?"

Kai read the note. Then he grinned. "Beats me. Let's get some of those big apples."

"It has to mean something," Serena said.

"No clue. We can ask April and Troy. Maybe they have some idea. Or maybe he just wants you to talk to him again."

"Yeah."

Serena wasn't convinced. Ollie was strange. But that didn't mean the note was a lie. Serena didn't want to ask Ollie about it. That would mean a whole new round of weirdness.

Still, maybe there was another way.

CHAPTER 10

ON THE TRAIL

Serena asked April. Her best girlfriend had nothing to add. She talked to Troy and Megan too. They each had nothing. They shared Kai's point of view. Ollie was an oddball. There was nothing for him to forgive Kai for.

"Let's just think about the party," April said.

Serena couldn't get Ollie's note out of her mind. Not that she saw him or heard from him. No calls. No texts. She didn't see him in the woods when she walked Toots. It was like he had disappeared. She wondered if that was a sign. Maybe she should just move on.

But she couldn't move on. What he had written bothered her too much. So she started to ask around. She went into the town library. Mrs. Peters worked in the children's section.

"Hi, Mrs. Peters. Have you been working here a long time?"

"Ten years," said the librarian.

"Then maybe you can help me. I'm new here. I'm making friends. But are they really as nice as they seem? Ollie Kidd? Kai Lambert? Do you know them?"

Mrs. Peters smiled. "Ollie Kidd? I'll never forget him."

Serena perked up. "Really? How come?"

"He learned to read when he was in preschool. Used to come in with his mother to get books all the time," Mrs. Peters said. "Then he moved away."

"He's back in town," Serena said.

"Oh, great! If you see him, tell him I asked after

him. He needs to come in. We've got a lot of great new books." Mrs. Peters gave Serena the once-over. "You look like a reader too. Can I suggest some books for you? Tamora Pierce? Laurie Halse Anderson? How about David Lubar? He's pretty funny."

"What about Kai?' Serena asked. Books were not why she was there.

Mrs. Peters shook her head. "I'm afraid not. Do you have a picture of him?"

Serena had one on her phone. But Mrs. Peters didn't recall him. "I don't think he was ever in the library. Is he sporty? Maybe you'll want to talk to the head of the rec center. Mr. Chan. He knows all the boys."

"That's a great idea. Thanks, Mrs. Peters."

The librarian grinned. "Come back if you need a book. Or two books. Or a dozen books!"

The rec center was next door to the library. It had tennis courts outside. There was a basketball court inside. It also housed a pool, gym, and cardio room for exercise classes.

It wasn't hard to find Mr. Chan. His office was right inside the front door. Serena found him doing paperwork. He looked up when she tapped on the door.

"Hi there. How can I help you? You want to register for winter water polo?"

Serena shook her head. She was not athletic. "Not exactly. I … I've got this friend. He's a big sports guy." She made it up as she went along. "I want to get him a birthday present. I thought you might know him. Could you give me ideas? He told me he used to hang out here. I really don't know much about sports."

"I'm happy to help. What's this fellow's name?"

"Kai," Serena said. "Kai Lambert."

Mr. Chan's face clouded over. "Your friend is Kai Lambert?"

"Yeah." Serena got a bad feeling in her stomach from Mr. Chan's reaction. "Is that bad?"

Mr. Chan shrugged. "Might be. I don't know if I'm allowed to tell you this. I'm going to say it anyway. I kicked him out of the gym when he was in second grade."

"What? What for?"

"He played rough. Every game. Basketball. Flag football. Water polo. It was so wrong. He got multiple warnings. Too many fair chances. Finally I had to get tough."

Serena reeled a little. This didn't have anything to do with Ollie. But it didn't say much for her boyfriend. "How long was he barred for?"

"A year," Mr. Chan said. "He's the only kid I've ever barred. He never came back. Not that I mind. I can't really help you with that present."

"Actually?' Serena said. "It's very, very helpful. Thanks, Mr. Chan."

Serena left the rec center. But she wasn't any closer to the story of Ollie and Kai. She had learned a lot about her boyfriend. None of it was good.

CHAPTER 11

THE WHOLE STORY

On her way out of the rec center, she saw Troy. He was bouncing a basketball. Troy smiled when he saw her. "Hey, it's the great Serena. I was hoping to run into you sometime. Sorry again for that dust-up at the movies. What brings you here? Want to play water polo?"

Serena shook her head. She decided to be honest. "I was actually talking to Mr. Chan about Kai."

Troy whistled. "I bet that didn't go well. Kai

had his problems at this gym. Back in second grade."

"That's what Mr. Chan told me."

"Then he started playing music. Best thing that ever happened to him."

"He sounds like he was pretty mean back then," Serena said.

Troy sighed. "On the court, yeah. Look. Tell me the truth. Why are you snooping around?"

Serena decided to be honest. "I heard something about him and Ollie. I think maybe he did something to Ollie that hurt him. Kai won't say a word. And I really want to know."

Troy puffed a little air out. He bounced his basketball a few times. "Look, Serena. There's something I think you should know. I don't know if Kai would want me to talk about this. But I'm going to tell you anyway. Take a walk with me. I'll fill you in."

They walked from the rec center to town. Troy talked. Serena listened.

"Ollie was one of those kids who got bullied a lot," Troy said.

"Really?"

"He was weird back then. Never played games with the other kids. Kept to himself a lot of the time. Head always in a book. Who bullied him? Everyone. Everyone who didn't ignore him."

Serena felt her blood start to run hot. Was Kai one of the bullies? Ollie had forgiven him. It was a graceful thing to do.

"Was Kai one of the bullies?" Serena asked.

Troy frowned. They walked toward the town square. "Well, that's just the thing. He never bullied Ollie. Not even one time."

Serena felt a wave of relief flood her soul. But there was still doubt. "I don't get it. Why is Ollie so freaked out?"

They were outside Blizz. Troy stopped. He faced Serena. "Here's the thing, Serena. Ollie wanted Kai to be his friend. Kai wasn't interested. He wasn't going to be mean to Kai. That didn't mean he wanted to hang out with him. Let's face it. The dude is kind of off. Ollie got pissed. Very pissed, in fact. But one person can't make another like him. Life doesn't work that way."

"Wow!" Serena said. "That's some story."

"Yeah," Troy said.

There was still one thing that bugged Serena. It was what Mr. Chan had said about Kai's temper.

"Can I ask you something else?"

Troy nodded. "Yeah. Anything."

"Mr. Chan said Kai always played rough. Is that true?"

Troy nodded. "It's true. And you know what? I think the best person to ask about it is Kai."

Serena and Kai had a social studies test. Kai wasn't all that big on school. But she had insisted he come over to study. They were at the kitchen table with their books spread out. The test was on World War II.

"You're going to turn me into a student," Kai joked.

"Try it. You might like it."

Kai found a banana and peeled it. "Doubtful."

"You know, Troy talked to me today," Serena said. She felt nervous even to bring this up.

"About what?"

"You and Ollie. Back in first grade. How everyone bullied him but you. How he got mad because you didn't want to be his friend."

"It was a long time ago. We were all just kids." He bit off a small piece of banana.

"Some memories last a long time. I guess that one did for Ollie. I just want to say, I think you did the right thing." Serena scrunched up her face. "Why didn't you just tell me?"

Kai chewed some more. "Well, you know me. I don't want to toot my own horn."

Huh? That was a strange thing to say. Serena had never taken Kai to be modest. Maybe he was just being modest about this. "Can I ask you one more thing?"

"Why not?"

Serena didn't want there to be secrets between them. So she told him what she had done. She admitted she'd gone to the rec center and the library. "I'm sorry. I'm nosy."

Kai grinned. "You're *Serena CSI*. Like a TV show."

"Funny. Anyway, Mr. Chan said you were a rough player. Very rough."

"Yep. Asked to leave the rec center." Kai blushed a little. "I guess divorce can mess a kid up. My parents had split up that year. I kind of took it out on others. I'm not proud of it."

Serena was proud of him. He'd told her the truth. It didn't make him look good, but it was what had happened. It all made sense. She leaned over and kissed him. He kissed her back.

One kiss turned to two. Two turned to four.

And four might have turned to eight. But they were at the kitchen table. Serena was the one who slowed things down. But she did it with a smile.

"You're good at that." Then she frowned. "I bet you had a lot of practice."

Kai grinned. "Only on my pillow."

"That's a lie. But I'll go with it," she said.

She sat back in her chair, feeling great. She wished that everyone could feel as good as she did. Even Ollie. That gave her an idea.

"What would you think about inviting Ollie to the party on Friday night? He probably wouldn't come. I bet it would mean a lot to him."

"You really want that?" Kai asked. "Things are cool with him now. I still think every time you contact him, it gives him false hope. You want to start up all over again?"

"It won't be like that. It's just a nice thing to do. What do you think?" She gave Kai her best and biggest grin. "Please?"

Kai sighed. "Well, it's your party. But I'm telling you. This is not a good idea."

Serena leaned close to him. "I'm going to prove you wrong."

Then she kissed him again.

CHAPTER 12

JUMPED

Serena texted an invite to Ollie. He texted back that he'd love to come.

SERENA: What's your costume going to be?

He took a moment to respond.

OLLIE: Beats me. Maybe an alien. Some say I am one already.

SERENA: (Stop that! Ur cool.)

OLLIE: (Does Kai know about this?)

Serena fibbed a little bit for a good cause.

SERENA: (Ollie? It was both our idea.)

He sent back a happy face.

OLLIE: (Anything I can bring?)

SERENA: (Just yourself.)

OLLIE: (Gr8. Till Friday.)

As it turned out, she saw him before Friday night.

By Thursday afternoon everything was set. The decorations were up. The food was ordered. The sound system was checked. Even the bonfire was ready for a match. April had been a big help. So had Kai and Troy. The work had gone by so fast that it barely seemed like work at all.

The weather for Friday was supposed to be perfect too. Clear skies. Temps in the high sixties. No wind. It would be a great night for a party.

With nothing else to do, she took Toots to the dog park after school. That's where she saw Ollie and Petey. They were walking toward the doggie playground. To her surprise, Ollie was limping. She ran over to him. Toots and Petey danced around each other, happy to be reunited. Ollie seemed to force a smile.

"What happened to you? Were you in an accident?" Serena asked.

Ollie frowned. "Not even close. I would say it was on purpose."

"What?" Serena was confused.

"It was no accident," Ollie said. "I got jumped."

"*What?* When? *How?*"

Ollie told the story. The night before, he had been walking Petey near the woods. It was dark. He didn't have a flashlight. He got attacked from behind. He was pushed to the ground. Then kicked in the leg. Nothing was broken, but the leg was sore.

This was horrible. She fired questions at him. "Who did it? Did they say anything? Did you go to the police?"

"No clue. No police. No point. I don't even know if it was one person or more. Someone did yell something at me. I didn't know the voice. Maybe it was faked." Ollie sounded tired. Sad.

"What did he say?"

"He?" Ollie asked. "Your bias is showing."

"Ollie? Get a grip! We can talk about bias another time. *What was said?*"

Ollie managed a grin. "For what it's worth, I think it was a guy. He told me to get out of town. He called me 'a human stain.' "

Serena gritted her teeth. "That's so ugly. It's also not true."

"I'm used to it."

The more Serena thought about what had happened to Ollie, the madder she got. "Don't be afraid of the party. I want you to come. I think you need to come. I'll talk to Kai. We'll make sure you're safe. I swear it."

Ollie watched the dogs for a moment. Finally he turned back to Serena. "Look. There's something I need to say to you. I don't think you're going to like it. It's about Kai."

CHAPTER 13

BITTER TRUTH

There was so much going on in the dog park. But none of it mattered to Serena. What mattered was what Ollie needed to tell her.

"Just say it," she told Ollie. "Whatever it is. I can handle it."

Ollie bit his lower lip. "Okay. Here's the thing. Your boyfriend was a bully. The worst. He made my life hell. He'd call me names. He would push me. I was a living target. I hated every minute of every day. He never let up. That nickname they call me? Oddball? That was his idea. Think of what that feels like. To come to school every day and have the kids call you that. It made me sick. Not just in my head, but in my heart. I'd throw up in the bathroom. Why did we leave town? Kai is why. I hate to have to tell you this. But it's all true."

Serena felt dizzy. Her legs were weak. She forced herself to stand up straight.

"That's not what he told me. He said he was nice to you. That he stopped people from bullying you. He said you wanted to be his friend, but he wasn't into it."

"He's a liar," Ollie said.

"Why?" she asked. "Why would he do that to you?"

Ollie shrugged. "You'd have to ask him. I think he was just mean in his bones. I think maybe he still is."

Serena shook her head. Something didn't add up. "No. It doesn't make sense. *You* wanted to be our friend. *You* wanted to hang out with him. If he did that to you, why would you want to get all buddy-buddy?"

His answer was simple. "I wanted to see if he was sorry. To see if he'd say something. He didn't. He didn't even come close." Ollie edged closer to Serena. "Look. Everyone has done stuff they're sorry for. That's why we're human, not God. But if you don't own the past, you can never move into the future. Serena, I'm sorry to have to tell you all this. I know you like the guy. But he's bad news."

Serena took some deep breaths. It was possible. Kai had those problems at the rec center. But she knew a lot of kids who had been in class with Kai and Ollie in first grade. None of them had said Kai was a bully. They all said he was fine.

"How can I know this is true?" she asked him.

"Serena, I have no reason to make this up."

"I wasn't there. How can I believe it if I wasn't there? I'm hearing different stuff from different people. You're saying Kai lied to me. I want to be sure."

"I have an idea."

Serena raised her eyebrows. "Yeah?"

He nodded gravely. "Our teacher was Miss Posner. She's retired. But she still lives in town. I can take you to talk to her. She knows everything."

"I'd like that."

But Serena knew she would not like it. It didn't matter. She had to get to the truth. Serena couldn't let it go until she knew.

Two hours later, Serena was waiting for Kai in Blizz. She'd texted him. Told him she had to talk to him. He asked what it was about. She said they had to talk face to face.

When he came into Blizz, he was all sunshine. "Hey, my girlfriend. What's up? Need more help with the party tomorrow? I'm there if you need me. Just say what you need done."

"Sit," she said firmly.

He did. "What's the matter?"

"I met someone today I think you know," she said.

"Who?"

This was *so* hard.

"Miss Posner. She taught you in first grade. Ollie too."

Kai laughed. "Posner? That old bag? I thought she was dead. How'd you meet her?"

"She isn't old. She's in her sixties. And she isn't a bag. She's nice. What she told me about you back in first grade? That wasn't so nice. I think you know what I mean."

She could almost see steam coming out of Kai's ears. He was so upset.

"Oh. I get it. She said stuff about Ollie and me. Why you'd talk to her anyway? Did he tell you to? *Oddball?*"

Serena didn't want to get into it. Just this

talk was hard enough. She stood. "Look, Kai. Do everyone a favor. Don't come to my party tomorrow. We're through."

"Over something that happened back in first grade?!" Kai was livid.

"No. You're a liar. And don't talk to me again. I don't like liars."

CHAPTER 14

THE PARTY

There was buzz the next day. Kai and Serena were through. Everyone knew they had split up. Everyone knew why. What was amazing to Serena was the number of people who came up to her. They said they'd known what a bully Kai had been back in first grade. They just thought that he'd changed. They thought there had been no reason to tell her.

It gave Serena a hard choice. Stop being friends with all of them. Or let it go. She decided to let it go. Except for Troy. She just couldn't. He had lied to protect Kai. She told him not to come to the party either. He'd shrugged. Said okay.

The hardest talk was with April. It happened in the restroom right before lunch.

"Why didn't you tell me?" Serena asked. It was more an accusation than a question.

"I swear I didn't know," April said.

"How is that even possible?" Serena dug her brush out of her bag. She fake-brushed her hair just for something to do.

"I don't know. I was six, Serena. I had other friends. Really. I didn't pay any attention to the boys."

"What about the nickname?" Serena asked. "Everyone knew about it. That had to come from someplace!"

"Well, yeah. Because he was *odd*."

Serena made a decision. "I want to be your friend. I want to throw this party with you. But there's something I need you to do for me first."

April's face was open. "I still want to be your friend. Tell me what I can do."

Serena took out her phone. Then texted Ollie's number to April. "I just sent you his digits. Call Ollie and tell him not to worry. Tell him he'll be fine at the party. We'll all be watching out for him."

April put out her hand for a shake. "I'm all over it."

Serena skipped the handshake. Instead, she hugged her friend. It was good to know that April was a good egg.

The party rocked. Serena wore the red devil costume. April dressed as a pirate. As Serena looked around her backyard, she saw more great costumes. Charlie Chaplin. Ghosts. Katniss Everdeen, of course. A piece of sushi. Four friends had come as spring, winter, summer, and fall. There had to be twenty or twenty-five people all dressed up.

Ollie said he would come as a space alien.

He wasn't there yet, though. That was fine. Serena knew she had done the right thing with Kai. He wouldn't dare show up. Neither would Troy. They could have their own party. There was pumpkin carving. There was bobbing for apples. Everyone was having fun.

A boy dressed as a NASCAR driver stepped in front of her. He wore a helmet too. "Great party," he said. "Thanks for inviting me."

He took off the helmet. Serena saw it was a guy named Brian. He was in her Spanish class. The star student, in fact.

"I'm glad you're here," she said.

"Great costume too. You look like a devil. Except you're an angel in disguise."

Serena blushed. Yep. No doubt about it. The guy was flirting with her.

"I'm glad you decided to dump Kai," he said. "He's bad news."

"I don't really want to talk about him. It's over. But I don't get why he has so many friends."

"Because most people are just chicken. They don't want Kai to turn on them. They don't want to be the next kid with a nickname." Brian pointed to some kids dancing. "Wanna dance?"

Serena saw April with another guy from Spanish class. His name was Alex. He was a great dancer. The floor cleared off so he could bust a few moves. People egged him on. April was a good dancer too. When the song ended, there were whoops and cheers.

Then April quieted the crowd. "Okay! Okay! Big cheer for our host. She's new in town. We're glad she's here. Go, Serena!"

There was a ton of clapping. Serena felt great. It was one more sign that she was part of her new school. It meant a lot to have friends. Moving was scary. She wondered what it had been like for Ollie. He'd had to leave school because he had no friends. Then he never got a chance to make any. It didn't matter if he was a little weird. Who wasn't a little weird? Normal was boring.

That's when she saw someone come into the backyard in a space alien costume. She was happy. It was Ollie. No. Not Ollie. And not one person in an alien outfit. *Four* people.

What the heck?

Serena went right over to them. "Who are you?"

One of the aliens whipped off his mask. It was Troy. He was crashing her party. That meant the other aliens had to be too. For sure one of them was Kai.

CHAPTER 15

BEHIND THE MASK

April, Brian, and Alex joined Serena as she confronted Kai. It never hurt to have backup. She felt safe as she got in Troy's face. "You aren't invited. Who are these other guys?"

Troy laughed. "We're from the planet Lovetron. Can't you tell? Dudes, unmask!"

They whipped off their masks. These guys didn't even go to their school. Stupid Troy! He had set up a group party crash.

Serena's eyes narrowed to slits. "You need to

leave," she said. "Now! Before I get my parents. The cops. Both. Wait! Where's Kai? And who told you to dress as aliens?"

She was worried about Ollie. How did they know to dress as aliens? It was no accident. Where was Ollie?

"That's for us to know. And you not to find out." Troy turned to his friends. "Let's go!"

With loud screams, they ran through the party and out to the street. Good riddance! But where was Ollie? Where was Kai?

Serena turned to April, Alex, and Brian. "I need you guys to come with me."

She texted her parents. She was going to look for Ollie. Then, without waiting for response, she ditched her own party.

April and Alex took off in one direction. Serena and Brian headed in another. Then Serena heard Kai's voice before she saw him.

"Why'd you come back here? Why'd you get

between my girlfriend and me? I'm going to tear you to pieces. You'll wish you never came back."

Serena called into the night. "Kai? Are you with Ollie? If you are, back off!"

Curse words came back at her from the darkness.

"Where are you, Ollie?" Serena yelled.

"Over here!" he cried.

Serena sent a quick text to her parents. Then she and Brian tried to follow the sound of Ollie's voice with their cellphones' flashlights.

They spotted him quickly. Ollie was in his costume. Kai stood over him. He had Ollie backed up against a fence. Ollie was trapped.

Serena and Brian hustled over.

"Back off, Kai," Serena said.

"Or what, Serena? You're going to break up with me? You already did!"

With a wild scream, Kai rushed at Ollie. Serena and Brian were on him in a second. Kai was strong, but the two of them plus Ollie were stronger. Kai kicked and yelled as they tried to hold him down.

A few seconds later more people arrived. Also, Serena's parents. It was only then that Kai stopped throwing punches. Serena's parents called the police. Several patrol cars soon showed up. By that time, most of the party had moved to the street to watch the action.

"Show's over," Serena said as the cop car with Kai in it moved off. "There's a lot more party ahead. I'm upping the best costume prize to fifty bucks!"

She gulped at her own words. Fifty bucks was about as much cash she had in the world. But she wanted to save the party.

Her father stepped up next to her. "Good job. On everything. We'll cover you for that money."

Serena gave her dad a hug.

Thirty minutes later, the costume contest was underway. Votes were secret. April and Alex were counting the ballots. Serena had voted for April.

Mostly, she'd been watching Ollie. Kids tried to be nice to him. That was good.

Ollie saw her watching him. He came over. "Thanks for finding me before. You saved my butt."

"You were right about Kai," she said. "I wish I could have seen it myself."

"Everyone has a mask they live behind," he said. "What's yours?"

Serena shrugged. "Beats me."

"Think about it. Then get back to me." Ollie moved away.

"Yahoo! We have a winner," April yelled.

The kids gathered around. Who would win the fifty dollars? April stood on a chair to make the announcement. "Our winning costume is Brian James!"

The kids cheered. Brian whipped off his helmet. Then he stepped over to April. Serena had put a crisp fifty-dollar bill in an envelope. April handed the envelope to Brian. The crowd cheered again.

It was time for the bonfire. Serena's dad lit it. Everyone gathered around. Serena thought about Ollie's words. There were all these people in masks. But those weren't the kind of masks Ollie was talking about.

Ollie was who he was. Real. He didn't hide behind a mask. He put it all out there. It wasn't a bad way to be. She looked at Brian. He'd put his helmet back on. Was Brian hiding anything? Serena really liked him. But she didn't really know him. Kai wore a mask she never imagined. Maybe Brian did too.

Brian waved the envelope with the money. Then he grinned at her. She waved back. He didn't seem like the kind of guy who'd be hiding something. But neither had Kai.

She wanted a friend first. There would be time for another boyfriend. Was Brian hiding anything? Before she went any further with him, she vowed to herself that she would find out.

WANT TO KEEP READING?

9781680211443

Turn the page for a sneak peek at another book in the White Lightning series:

THE UNDERDOGS

CHAPTER 1

LUNCH GAME

Jasmine Le's eyes narrowed. She was watching Mark Kline play football. It was lunchtime. Mark and some other guys were playing.

A blond thirteen-year-old god. Wow! she thought.

"Oh man!" Mark yelled. "You blew it."

He was looking at Mike Ramirez. Mike had missed a pass. The ball was on the ground. It had landed close to Jasmine.

Her BFFs were sitting on some bleachers behind her. Zoe Ebad and Tess Quade. Zoe was a tall and perfect blonde. "Do you ever get pimples? I've never seen one on your face. Unfair!" Tess once told her.

Tess's hair was long and brown. She had smooth dark skin.

Jasmine was a hybrid of the two. Long black hair. Olive skin.

Everyone on the field was in eighth grade. They went to Meadow Springs Middle School.

"Shouldn't you throw the ball back?" Zoe asked.

Jasmine wasn't a tomboy. But there were only boys on her street. She had played kickball with them. Baseball, soccer, and even tackle football too. She grabbed the football. Then she threw it back.

"Oh my gosh!" Zoe said, laughing. "You did it. I can't believe it."

"Did you think she wouldn't?" Tess asked.

The ball soared through the air. The boys watched it. Mark barely moved to catch it.

"Nice throw," Mark said. "For a girl."

"Nice throw, period," Jasmine said.

Mark laughed. "All right. Let's get in our formations," he called. "We still have fifteen minutes till the bell rings."

"Are you going to eat your lunch?" Zoe asked. She held up Jasmine's sandwich. "It looks good."

"Eat it," Jasmine said. "I'm going to play football."

Tess and Zoe looked at each other. "I don't recall them asking you to play," Tess said.

"So?" Jasmine smirked. She walked out onto the field. Jasmine planted herself between the two teams. The boys started yelling. She tuned it out. Mark stared at her. She didn't even blink.

"What are you doing?" Mark asked.

"I want to play football," Jasmine said. "I'm just as good as any of you."

"But you're a girl." Mark frowned. "You can't play football!"

"Why not? I play with boys a lot. I've even played tackle football."

"You're a girl!" Mark said again. "You will get hurt."

"No, I won't!"

The other boys yelled too. They told Jasmine to get off the field. Tess and Zoe ran over.

"Jasmine," Zoe said. "Come on!"

"Ignore our friend," Tess said to Mark. "She ate lunch in the cafeteria. Bad food makes you weird."

"I'm feeling fine," Jasmine said. "If boys can play football, we can too."

"Mr. Ross," the boys called.

Mr. Ross was in charge of school security. The man was short and stocky. He always wore tracksuits. Maybe he had played high school football. But he was out of shape now.

"What's the problem here?" Mr. Ross asked.

"Jasmine thinks she can get in on this game. Play football with us," Mark said.

"I *can* play football," Jasmine said. "They just won't let me."

Mr. Ross stared at them. "Um. Now listen, Jasmine." Mr. Ross stopped talking. He looked like he was thinking. "These boys are playing football. It's not the game for you."

"Why not?"

"Well. Um … because you're a girl."

"That's not a reason. Sex doesn't matter. I can play," Jasmine insisted.

"Get her off the field, Mr. Ross!" one player yelled.

"Look," Mr. Ross said. "You must get off—"

"No!"

Silence.

Mr. Ross was known for being nice. But he did have a temper. "Leave this field, or go see the principal. It's up to you."

Jasmine held her ground. But Zoe stepped

in. "We were just leaving," she said. Zoe grabbed Jasmine's arm. "Enjoy your game," she yelled to the boys.

Tess grabbed Jasmine's other arm.

The girls led her off the field.

The rest of lunch passed in silence. Jasmine sat on the bleachers with Tess and Zoe. She watched the game. What would it be like if she were allowed to play?

"Stop being so mad," Zoe said. "You want to play football? Since when?"

"Since those boys wouldn't let me," Jasmine said.

Jasmine fumed the rest of the day. No way would she take no for an answer. Girls could play football. They could if they wanted to play.

The friends met up after school. They always walked home together.

"Look," Tess said. "That shirt is so cute." Tess

showed the girls her phone. The cool shirt was on Instagram.

"Do you like it, Jazz?" Tess asked Jasmine.

Jasmine eyed the shirt. It was white. "I'm Not Hot" was written on it. "It's cool," Jasmine said.

But Jasmine kept thinking about football. Zoe and Tess talked. Jasmine thought about justice. Then something caught her eye. They were near Wagner Park.

There was Mark. Again. It was football practice. Looked like a Pop Warner team. She could see the team name. The Marauders.

Their coach was tall. He was dressed like Mr. Ross.

Jasmine had a thought. "Wait! I've got an idea," she said. She walked over to the field.

"Here we go again," Zoe said, rolling her eyes.